Kevin can see a very big cat.

The very big cat can
run very fast.

Kevin cannot run
very fast.

The very big cat can
run zig-zag, zig-zag.

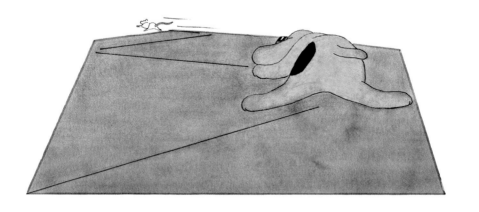

Kevin cannot run

zig-zag, zig-zag.

The very big cat runs
into a very big box.

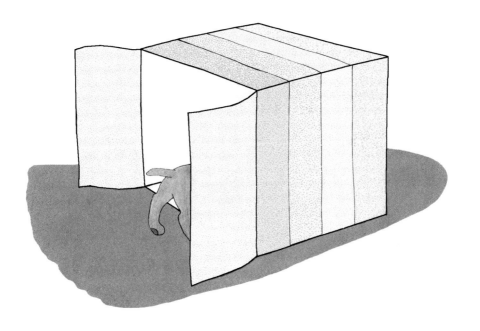

Kevin runs into the
very big box.

Look at Kevin and
the very big cat in
the very big box.